The Island of Serenity

Part 1
Destruction

Book 2

Sun & Rain

By
Gary Edward Gedall
01/01/2015

Published by:

From Words to Worlds

Lausanne, Switzerland

www.fromwordstoworlds.com

Images synthesized by Boris : contact@avasta.ch

ISBN: **2-940535-03-5**

ISBN 13: **978-2-940535-03-3**

About the Author

Gary Edward Gedall is a state registered psychologist, psychotherapist, trained in Ericksonian hypnosis and EMDR.

He has ordinary and master's degrees in Psychology from the Universities of Geneva and Lausanne and an Honours Degree in Management Sciences from Aston University in the UK.

He has lived as an associate member of the Findhorn Spiritual Community, has been a regular visitor to the Osho meditation centre in Puna, India. And as part of his continuing quest into alternative beliefs and healing practices, he completed the three-year practical training, given by the Foundation for Shamanic Studies in 2012.

He is now, (2014 – 2016), studying for a DAS, (Diploma of Advanced Studies), as a therapist using horses.

His hobbies are; writing, western riding and spoiling his children.

He is currently living and working in Lausanne, Switzerland.

Realization, Repentance, Redemption, Release & Rebirth

This book was inspired by the realization that I had never really mourned the death of my older brother, Lloyd, to whom series is dedicated.

In my therapy practice, I am all too often confronted with patients who feel that their lives no longer have any sense or perspective.
It is my job to help them find back the sense of their lives, and to encourage them in finding again some optimism that things can get better.

This book is for all of you that have made errors, mistakes, stupid and destructive choices and actions, (which should cover approximatively 99% of the world's population).

We have all got it wrong sometimes in our lives, but it is never too late to start to get it right.

Any form on self-harming, or life threatening acts are a crime against yourself; your God, (however you might name or experience 'it', even if you are feeling totally abandoned), and everyone that cares for you, (and there are always many more than you might feel at any moment).

Remember, you can always find teachers; therapists, spiritual and religious guides, etc., etc,. who are there to help you on your path. If you need help, don't hesitate to reach out, you don't have to face your demons alone.

I take also this opportunity to thank my daughter, Kyra for her help in the structuring of the series, and the time and interest that she invested in reflecting with me on the stories.

Gary, Lausanne 6th January 2015

The Island of Serenity Pt 1 Book 2 – Sun & Rain

Disclaimer:

Contents:

Book 1 – Survival (Abridged)

Book 2 -From Sun to Rain

Chapter 1

Sorry

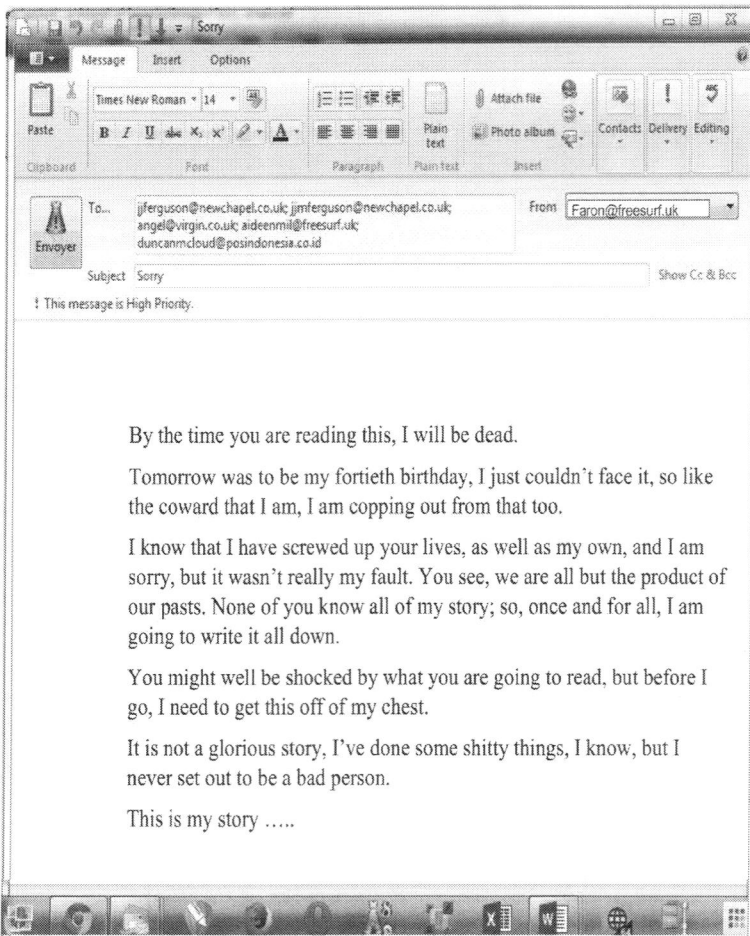

By the time you are reading this, I will be dead.

Tomorrow was to be my fortieth birthday, I just couldn't face it, so like the coward that I am, I am copping out from that too.

I know that I have screwed up your lives, as well as my own, and I am sorry, but it wasn't really my fault. You see, we are all but the product of our pasts. None of you know all of my story; so, once and for all, I am going to write it all down.

You might well be shocked by what you are going to read, but before I go, I need to get this off of my chest.

It is not a glorious story, I've done some shitty things, I know, but I never set out to be a bad person.

This is my story .....

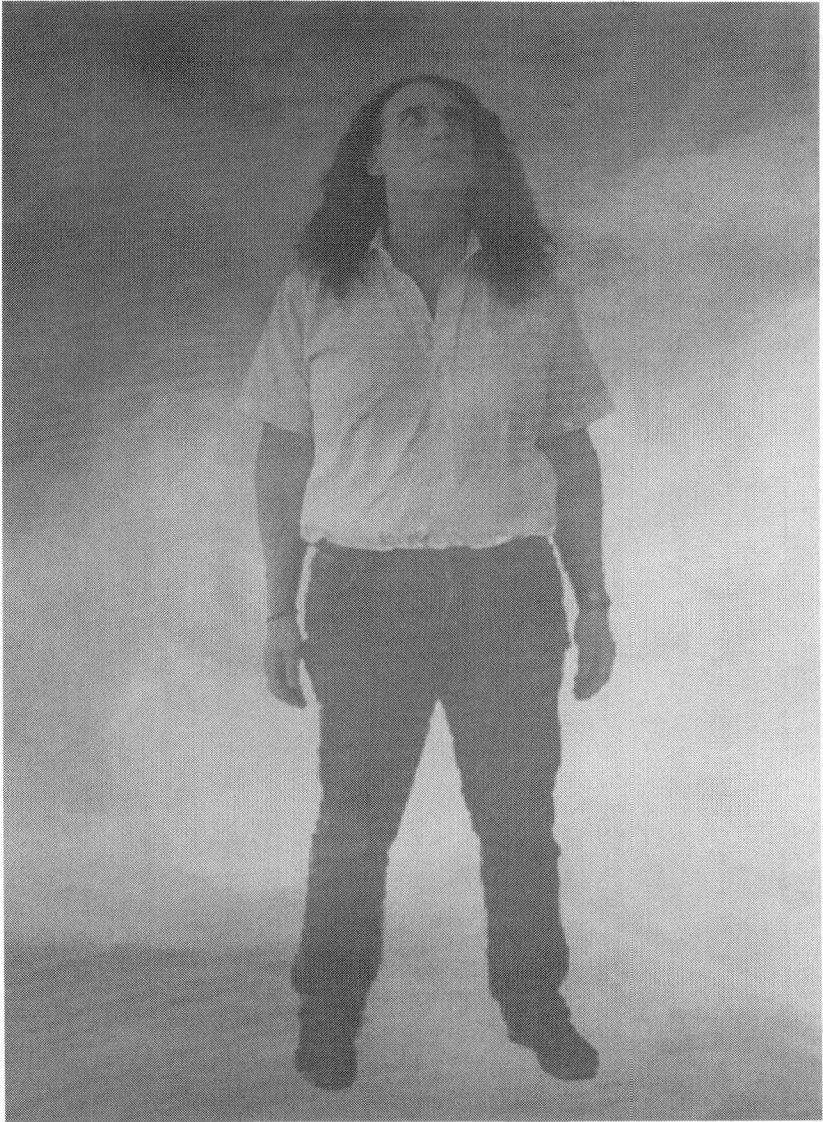

Chapter 2

Beginning: Limbo

There is fog or mist, or something; making everything unclear….

"Where the hell is this?"

"Not quite Hell, Faron."

"Who are you, where are you, how do you know my name?"

"Who I am is of no importance; where I am, is not here and I know your name because I am here to help you."

"But where am I, am I dead?"

"You are in-between."

"In-between what?"

"Here and there."

"Is this purgatory?"

"You might choose to call it that."

"Why am I here?"

"Why do you think?"

"Because you don't know where to send me?"

"Where you should go next, will have to be decided."

"But I can't change what I've done."

"You can change who you are now."

"But it's too late."

"If it was too late, there would be no point in you being here."

"Listen, whoever or whatever you are, it is too late, I've totally screwed up my life, there's no point in trying to change anything."

"Fine, then I hope that you like this scenery,…"

"There is no scenery, just clouds or fog."

"Because this is where you will stay…."

"For how long?"

"Until you accept to change."

"That's my choice. Stay or change?"

"Isn't it the only choice, to change, or stay the same?"

"To change or remain the same?"

"Change or remain the same."

"Okay, change it is."

"Change it is."

"Okay."

Chapter 3

The Early Years

Some children are born with a silver spoon in their mouths, I was born with one rammed up my arse. That way I could sit up straight, stand up straight and shine from within….

My mother was the direct descendent from an obscure French noble family. They had the good idea to take an extended vacation, with their English neighbours, so they could keep their heads, when all about them were losing theirs.

My father, James John Ferguson or J.J. Ferguson, as he was known to everybody had also come from a type of royalty, as popular myth would have it.

One of his direct ancestors was supposed to have been an illegitimate son of one of the King James's.

His mother, in a bizarre type of mirroring of the story of my mother's family, (which is so unlikely that it could only be true), fed the young bastard with stories of his true nobility and of how, at some future moment in history, he would regain his true, noble status.

He came down to England and through hard work and careful money management, my father became, in his mid-thirties, one of the youngest factory owners ever. He was well on his way to becoming a wealthy man.

It was around this time that my father met my mother, who saw him as the perfect means to regain the noble status she had lost…

As soon as my mother fell pregnant with me, she searched for and found a distant, poor, French relative, a sort of maiden aunt, to come over and live with us. She was what they call a 'jeune fille au pair', although she was anything but a young girl, more than likely already in her late-forties or early fifties.

As a family member; plucked out of abject poverty, given a decent job, room, food, money, (actually not much more than pocket money really), my mother was confident that she would act in a serious and trustworthy manner.
In fact, Marie Madeleine did much more than that; she became a de facto mother substitute for me, caring for me, as she would if I had been the child that she never had.

This investment in me never wavered, even after the birth of my little brother Jean-Jacques Malcolm Ferguson two years and three months my junior.

It must be said that my earliest years were not unpleasant, with Marie Madeleine as my constant surveillant. Jean-Jacques became more and more a playmate, as the years progressed.

As for my parents I saw them mainly but in passing moments, we might cross my mother, ('Maman', as she preferred that we called her), in the morning, as we were preparing to go out somewhere.

'Bonjour mes chers, tout se passe bien?'

'Oui, Madame, tout va très bien. Et vous, Madame ?'

'Ça va, ça va, je suis très occupée. Soyez sages, mes enfants'.

'Oui, Maman.'

'Bonne journée.'

As you might probably have noticed, mother would speak to us in French; this was intentioned for us to acquire French as a mother tongue. The choice to have imported Marie-Madeleine, who only spoke French, was clearly part of this particular project.

'Where is Marie-Madeleine?'

'Elle ne travaille plus chez nous.'

'What ? Since when ?'

'Vous êtes grands, vous n'avez plus besoin d'elle. C'est réglé.'

I waited until J.J. returned that evening.

'Is it true that Marie-Madeleine has been sacked?'

'Aye lad, she's gone.'

'Just like that, like an old sock? After all that she's done for us?'

'Your mother has decided that she is no longer useful, so she was given notice. After all, she was only an employee….'
'No, she wasn't! She was family…. she IS family.'

'I'm sorry Jamie, (he rarely called me by my middle name), but it was your mother's decision. I just deal with the formalities.'

'But what will she do?'

'Oh I wouldn't worry too much on her behalf, she has a fine head on her shoulders. I've been thinking for some time that the factory would do well to have its own nursery.

Your mother has some friends that are looking to take some classes in French, both for themselves, and for their children. Marie-Madeleine is not likely to starve!'

I was not at all placated; full of anger and righteous indignation, despite the lateness of the hour, I threw on my coat and ran over to her little house.

I did knock before rushing in, but only just.

'Why hello Pierre-Alain. Qu'est ce qui se passe?'

'I just found out that you have been …', I didn't get to finish my sentence, for I had just noticed that she wasn't alone.

'Oh, please let me introduce my new neighbour, Muriel Miller and this is her daughter, Angelique.

And this crazy, young man, is the closest thing that I have to a son, Pierre-Alain James Ferguson.'

(This was the first time that I'd ever heard her speak English, but that wasn't to be the greatest shock of the evening).

I stiffly shook the hand of the lady, 'a pleasure.' I then turned to the young woman, true to her name, here, facing me was an honest to God angel.

'Hi', it was all that I could manage, I turned and ran out of the house as fast as I could, I felt like I was going to be sick.

Chapter 4

The Island of Survival

The fog starts to lift, he finds himself on a barren rock; behind, the sea is violently attacking the shoreline, smacking it savagely with a blind rage, as if its very presence was somehow an affront to its right to dominate the earth.

In front, there is a rough plane, with patches of vegetation, which are somewhere wrong, but he cannot make out exactly why, for the moment.

Further inland, he can see an enormous forest; a forest the like he had never seen or maybe heard of. The trees are huge, yes a few majestic redwoods maybe, but this was a whole forest of them, as far as the eyes could see.

The wind tests to see if he is capable of flight. It almost succeeds to lift him off the ground, but it is still not quite strong enough, so it gives that up.

Frustrated, it pushes him heavily to the hard rocky floor.

So, here he lays, angry and hurt. He rolls over onto his back, he looks up and a little back. 'What the???'

'Something wrong?'

'Everything is wrong, but the sky and the sun…'

'Ah'.

'Why is the sun red, and the sky turquoise?'

'Why is anything the way it is? I believe that it has something to do with the composition of the atmosphere.'

A shadow softly crosses over his face, from behind, cutting off the sun.

'What the …?' He turns and sits up, the figure is short and heavy set, somewhere a cross between a man and a small gorilla, wearing some sort of animal skin, to protect his privates. 'Is that you?'

'To ask if I am, who I am, is a question that warrants not a response.'

'But what are you?'

'The same as you.'

'You must be joking, you look like some kind of missing link.'

'Why not take a moment to look at your own hands?'

'My hands? Oh-my-God, these are not my hands.' They are short, wide, heavy, strong and very hairy, the finger nails black and claw like.

'They are now.'

'What have you done to me?'

'You are on the island of survival, here you will learn … how to survive.'

'But, I know how to survive.'

'What do you know?'

'I need to make a hut, start a fire.'

'Start a fire, quite right, and how do you start a fire?'
'I, I, I don't remember. How can I not remember how to make a fire?'

'Remind me, what's a wheel?'

'Stupid question, a wheel is a … it's a … a … thing.'

'What does it do?'

'I can't remember, I can't remember. What the Hell have you done to me?'

'This is a representation of a period of history, sort of like the stone age.'

'I know what the stone-age is. How can I remember that, but not what a wheel is.'

'This is like a sort of a dream; sometimes we know things that we didn't know, sometimes we can't even remember our own names.'

'What's the point of all this?'

'As I have said, you are to relearn to survive.'

'Like this?'

'Like that.'

'So, what do I need to do so that I can get out of here?'

'Hunt, kill, protect yourself.'

'And if I don't?'

'Then you will get hungry, cold, wet and maybe hurt.'

'But I cannot die, I can't get hungry or hurt.'

'Can you feel hunger and pain, in a dream?'

'So if I don't do the things that you want, then I will suffer?'

'I don't care what you do or don't do, but if you don't do the things that are necessary for survival, yes, you will suffer.'

'Will you help me?'

'I am only here to help.'
'Great, let's get started then.'

'I am sorry, we seem to have a slight misunderstanding. I am here to help you, in, how should I put it, in a sort of advisory capacity. For the practical stuff, sorry, you're rather on your own.'

'And exactly what would you advise me to be doing, in your advisory capacity, if I might dare to ask?'

'Of course, well, as the sun tends to heat up these rocks, rather a lot by the afternoon, maybe it would be, not a bad idea, to go a seek out some shade.'

He gets up, turning to the forest, 'how far do you think it is to the forest?'

There is no answer, he turns back towards the man, but he is no longer there.

'Great', and with that, the short, stubby man creature, starts to make his lumbering way to the protection of the forest.

'I say one thing for this thing of a body, Jimmy boy, it's bloody fit. Jimmy boy?

 How long since I've thought of myself as Jimmy boy? How long since I've been talking t' me-self?

Okay, just this stretch of red sand, it is bloody red, isn't it? Bloody red, like that; quite clever really.

I'm starting to get hot. My feet hurt. I should do something about that. I'm sure I know something so that me feet don't hurt on the hot ground; maybe I'll remember later. Just keep going. I'm nearly there. Nearly there…. okay, that's better, good forest, cool on the feet.'

'What the hell am I doing? What warped, sick game is he playing at? Anyway, who is he? Maybe it's just a creation of my own unconscious, that's what it must be!

I'm dying or dead, and I've created some sort of fantasy reality, so as to deal with the guilt of committing suicide.

Well, I'm not going to play anymore. I didn't want to live anymore, and I've no interest in some sort of experience of atonement.

Listen God, if this is your idea, sorry but I'm not interested; if I'm to go to Hell, well it's no more than I deserve! Just stop this charade, and let's get on with it!'

He waits for a response, a reaction- but nothing happens.

'Well, I'm going to make myself comfortable in this tree, and when you get bored, then you can do what you want.'

He does as he promises, climbs a tree and settles himself to wait. Sometime later he stirs himself....

'Shit, even if I'm dead, I need to pee.'

He descends the tree, and relieves himself.

'What's that?! What's there? Oh-my-God!'

The creatures resembles a huge bear.

'It surely can't hurt me; I'm not really here.'

He stands facing the great beast, undecided whether to climb back up the tree, run, or trust in his logic of being un-damageable. The beast advances, surprisingly quickly for such a massive creature.

His indecision has given the bear the moment that it needed. Before he can move, it swings its right paw and he is propelled from the ground.

He lands heavily, several feet away. It has struck him on the upper right arm, which is already painful and bleeding….

The blow has also winded and disorientated him, and he lays on the soft ground.

Watching the beast advance towards him, he is unable to react other than curl up into a ball, and experience the rising panic of being in an impossible situation with no possible means of escape.

Suddenly, there are loud screams, and a shower of stones lands on the bears' enormous furry body. It turns, screams back in anger and in pain, searching for the source of this outrage….

Again more screams from the trees, another rain of missiles, and the bear turns and runs off, whether to attack the stone throwers or to escape them, he cannot guess.

That the bear has left; that is the only information of any interest.

Some moments pass before anything else happens. Then, from somewhere out of the trees, a figure emerges. It resembles the form of the other man, but it is not him.

'Duncan, it's you! What are you doing here?'

The short, squat humanoid continues towards him. He looks at the fallen man and grunts.

'How can you be Duncan? You don't look like Duncan, but I know that you are him, weird.'

The other man still continues to advance cautiously towards him. The similarity to a gorilla is troubling.

He hesitates before coming close enough to contact. Then, very slowly, he reaches out his stubby hand to take the injured arm and examine it.

He moves it gently. He is testing whether it is broken or not……

….. 'You see, survival, is not every man for himself, or the survival of the fittest. Survival is a group concern; if your group, tribe, team do well, then you can also do well.'

'Survival is for team players.'

'There, now you've got it.'

'But do you think that it will be okay if Angelique stays with me?'

'Oh, you might do even better than her.'
'What do you mean?'

'Come, and I will show you.' He takes Faron by the hand and leads him into the darkness behind one of the huts. As they come out …

'Careful, you don't want to fall into a canal.'

'Canal?'

'Yes, Venice is full of them …

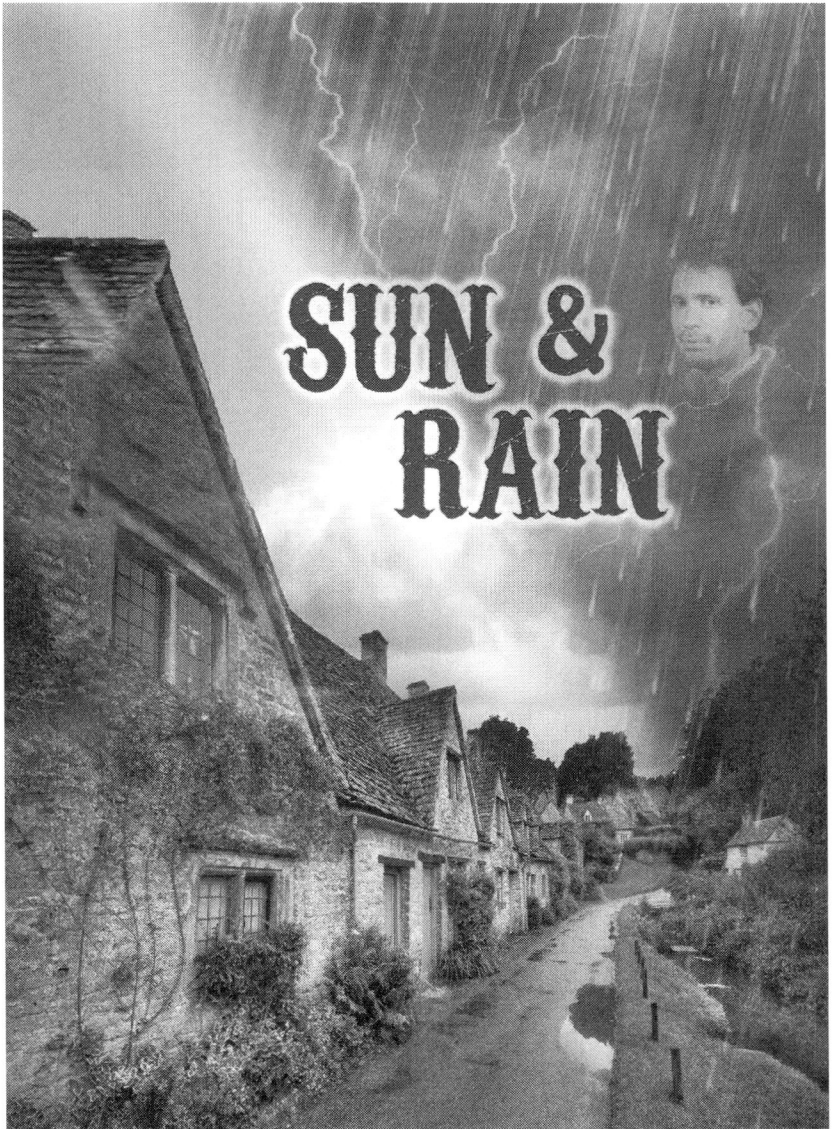

Chapter 5 In The Series

From Sun to Rain

Chapter 1

The Cat Out of the Bag

I immediately forgot my anger against my parents for throwing Marie Madeleine out. She very quickly found work, and even if she couldn't have earned that much, never seemed to want for anything.

Of course, her home was always open to me, and I visited very, very often. If my mother remarked anything at all, it didn't trouble her more than that.

This is, until she found out that it wasn't only to visit my old nurse that I was so often absent from home. Naturally, it was Jay's fault. During one of our Friday night dinners, when J.J. was present and reasonably sober, he decided to rile me on the subject of girls.

Up until the meeting with Angelique, I had always been particularly shy with the members of the fairer sex. I had, had little or no contact with any girls until starting school, so I'd never learned how to relate to them.

This made me more than just a little awkward and, as I said, very shy.

With Angelique it was very different.

We didn't talk much in those early years, which was to say that we didn't talk about things, (not that we really communicated that much more later on, for that matter – unfortunately). Frankly, we didn't have to.

Often I would help out Marie Madeleine with some practical chores.

Angelique would just sit or stand, silently watching me, playing absently with her mass of mad, copper hair. Or we'd sit, often on the postage stamp of a lawn of the house, sharing a simple picnic of supermarket biscuits and juice.

I'd tell her of all the wonderful things that I was going to do with my life, actually with our lives, even if it was never explicitly stated.

Or, later on in the evenings, (usually Saturday nights, or during holidays), I would read to my old nurse, who found reading increasingly tiring, classics in French; Molière, Maupassant, Hugo, Balzac, Zola.

Angelique would sit silently, absorbing it all in.

In fact, Marie Madeleine was also teaching her French; a fact that I was not to become aware of until some-time after.

So my father, having no knowledge of my sudden comfort and connection with the female of our species, was having a little fun, entertaining himself at my expense.

'Still a little shy with the ladies, are we? Still no, what do you call it, Antoinette? Oh 'petit ami'?

'Petite amie', my mother coldly corrected him, clearly emphasising the importance of the 't' and the final 'e' sound, which my poor father, couldn't even properly perceive.

'Right, petittt ami-y,' he turned, smiling to me, 'still stuttering every time that you have to talk to one?' It is true that when I was really nervous, I did have a slight tendency to stutter.

'Même pas vrai,' I suppose that Jean Jacques was somewhere thinking that he was protecting me.

'What's that, lad?'

'Pierre-Alain has a girl-friend, and her name is Angelique.'

'Is that so?' J.J. actually seemed quite pleased with this revelation. Which was more than could be said for my mother's reaction!

'C'est quoi cette bêtise? Who is this girl? Where do you know her from?'

Jean Jacques was about to continue to divulge the smallest details of my private life, when he chanced to look over in my direction.

He must have been able to read the hostility in my face, as even though he opened his mouth, not a sound escaped his head, not even a whisper.

'Well?' J.J. was not angry as Maman was. He just seemed inquisitive, he was looking full at me.

'Her name is Angelique, and she is the next door neighbour of Marie Madeleine. She's one year younger than me.'

'And what does her father do?' The chill in her voice could have turned Niagara Falls into a curtain of stalactites, in mid-summer.

'I suppose that he works in the factory, doesn't everybody?' I responded dully.

'I will not have my son cavorting with the daughter of a factory worker!'

'I used to be a factory worker!' It seemed that J.J. was sticking up for me, although it was more likely that he was just feeling belligerent, and was using that as a means to attack Maman.

She didn't reply; she didn't have to. You see, when my mother decided on something, it was almost guaranteed that it would come about! J.J. had long since realised that there were some battles that he just wasn't going to win.

After that subtle understanding had been reached, my mother had stopped arguing with him over these things, they both knew that it was just a waste of time and energy.

'We'll talk about it another time', was his way to move away from the subject and try and save a little face.

Jean Jacques knew that he had done a 'grosse bêtise', but it took him a while to understand exactly what; in the meantime, I made him suffer in every way that I knew how.

I hid his homework. I forced cook to stop making his favourite meals. I took messages for him, that I told him too late....

I told Maman, on a rare occasion that she stopped to talk to me, that he had decided that as soon as he could, he would stop learning French, and take up German!

However, my parents surprised me with their reaction. They didn't mention the discussion again. They didn't control my visits to Marie Madeleine, nor did they put, (as far as I could ascertain), pressure on Angelique or her parents, to limit our time together.

That left me with the opportunity of taking my life into my own hands....

Chapter 2

Mapping out the Future

It was only after the school summer exams that the axe dropped.

'Your mother and I have some news for you both!' He was no less drunk than usual, but he was holding himself, physically and mentally, very stiffly. 'You will be going away to Richmond, Arizona to work on a ranch and to learn to ride American style, for most of the summer.'

Neither of us could believe what we were hearing. A whole summer in America, learning to be cowboys, and Maman's sacred classical English riding ignored. Had they both been exchanged for alien look-alikes?

'And when you return from your holidays,' now it was her turn, 'you will be pleased to know that you have both had the good fortune to have been accepted at St. Josephs' higher school.'

It was unusual that she would speak to us in English. I think that she wanted us to be sure that J.J. was totally in agreement with this, and that there could be question of the sense, being 'lost in translation'.

'I've never heard of any St. Joseph's school.' I was already starting to panic. I had almost forgotten that other dinner, only a few months before. 'Where is it?'

'It's in Scotland, laddie. A very good school, according to the reports I've had.'

'But I don't want to go away to school!' Poor Jay, now you're being punished for being a snitch! 'Please don't make me go, s'il vous plait Maman, je veux rester ici avec vous.'

'No, you can't stay here with us. I've discussed it with your mother, and we have decided that it's the best thing for both of you.'

If you might be wondering why my parents would insist that Jean Jacques also be sent away, you need to realise that for many small tasks, it was now me that had become responsible for him.

Looking after him in the evenings, seeing that he did his homework, that he cleaned his teeth and went to bed on time…. Even getting both of us up, in the mornings, was now my job.

If I was sent away to school, then either they would have to find and pay for someone to look after him, (out of my mother's 'allowance'), or she would have to take over those tasks.

Clearly, for her, if I was to go to boarding school, then he would also. (Not to forget that, that expense would come directly out of my father's account!).

Even through my rage and anger, there was a reaction that was stronger; it was as if I was being controlled by some far off puppet master.

I turned round to the snivelling, slob that had wrecked the best thing in my life. My arm moved out, my hand touched his shoulder, my mouth opened and these words escaped from my pinched lips: 'Don't worry, I'll look after you.'

His response was all anyone would ever to hope to have heard: 'I know…. you're my big brother'.

Those words now cut through my tortured soul, like the tormented banshee's scream. Not to pass either, his wet half-smile shining, hopefully through his child's tears.

You see you know when you hurt someone terribly, when you are aware that you have disappointed someone, straight through to their very depths of their soul.

If you are capable to own your own guilt, and I can no longer escape from my own, then it is the moments of softness and trust that return to haunt you. This was one such moment.

Chapter 3

Home On The Range

As it says in the Bible, it came to pass.

The summer was all that we could having expected it to be, both for the good and the bad. The work was really hard and demanding; we got up early, fed the horses, scooped up the manure with big shovels, pushed the wheelbarrows to the crap pile, (I named it that), and that was all before breakfast.

The food was crazy, I could say that we ate like horses, but of course, that was not the case, moreover, we ate like ogres.

Eggs, pancakes, toast, fresh toast, (egg bread for the English, pain perdu, as we knew it), sausages, steak, (even some times for breakfast!, if we were planned to have a day away from the ranch).

It was the first time that we were allowed to drink real coffee; strong, sweet coffee, not the weak, milky coffee, (renversé), that Maman allowed cook to make me on cold, winter mornings.

After that we might brush the horses for a while, clean the saddles, (so much bigger and heavier than the thin strip of punished leather that we were used to).

Riding western style has some fundamental differences from classical riding; the reins are held almost always 'long', keeping a constant tension on the horses' mouth for even a minute is fault enough to warrant a ten minute lecture on the abuse of animals.

I was once forced to put a bridle over my head and grab the bit between my teeth, for five whole minutes, with one of the other boys pulling on the reins, just so that I could 'experience the pull'.

Everyone thought it dreadfully funny, 'til the ranch foreman strolled over and suggested that maybe everyone would do well to take a turn, and for ten minutes each, then it was my turn to laugh.

The stirrups are hung much lower, and more of the leg is used to direct the horse, in fact, we were quickly taught how to ride without using the reins at all.

One of the young 'dudes', as they called us, asked if it was so we could shot rifles while galloping.

'No!', came the reply; it was so you could lasso cows and eat beans while on long trails.

The horses are incredibly quiet and well behaved, we would ride out to repair the fences and 'ground tie' the horses; that means that you can just leave the reins on the floor, (split reins of course, attached – looped reins can get caught in the horses hoof), and the horse just waits and grazes.

One of the young dudes made the mistake to try and attach his horse, by the reins, to a post, this is VERY DANGEROUS, (that was the scream of the ranch hand, looking after us), the boy was sent back to the ranch, and banned from riding for the rest of the camp.

It was good but tough; Jay didn't bug me much, as he was one of the younger kids, he and three others, of about the same age, were split off to do other things.

Strangely enough, what he seemed to have enjoyed a lot, was working in the kitchens, he said it was a hoot, and he became an expert on making dozens of varieties of delicious cookies.

We both knew that our visit to the ranch was J.J.'s way of buying us off, but it was a great experience, just the same.

Coming back to England was as bad as we expected it to be, it was cold and wet, it expressed our feelings exactly.

Chapter 4

Where the North Wind blows

We had only two nights at home before we were, unceremoniously, shipped off to Scotland.

Marie Madeleine looked much older than when I left her at the beginning of the summer, her eyes were not doing well, they seemed to have lost most of their colour, she was not young, even when she started working for the family, but now she really started to look old.

Maybe she had some sort of sickness, which nobody knew of, but she really didn't look well.

Angelique, also looked older, but this was a much more pleasant surprise, she was transformed into a beautiful, young woman. I could hardly keep my hands off her, but all she would allow me was some heavy kissing, and the occasional and accident caressing of her breasts, due to my in-habitual, clumsiness.

We didn't talk at all of my going, in fact, we didn't talk much at all.

We walked around the village, I dared to show her off, well knowing that Maman would quickly get to hear of it.

It was a type of challenge, a defiance of her rules, she might be winning this round, but life is long, and we shall overcome.

Marie Madeleine came to see us off, but Angelique was only noticeable by her absence.

Maman give us a lecture of how we were now the representatives of the family honour, and J.J. gave us both an envelope with quite a lot of money in it, I supposed that was usual.

To be totally honest, St. Josephs' wasn't that bad at all. The boys were all from quite well to do families; they were, (mostly), brought up to be quiet and polite.

Of course there were some arrogant snobs, but they were mostly foreigners' or even worse, 'les nouveaux riches'.

(I am not as a rule, at all racist, for my mother, anyone from a 'bonne famille', was to be respected and appreciated, all others were to be tolerated and kept at a distance – neither race nor religion came into the equation.

For J.J., there were only decent human beings and lazy, scum, again, race didn't count for much).

The food was good and plentiful, the bedrooms were okay, (four beds to a dorm), the house and school rules were fair and reasonable, the teachers were definitely much better than the village school.

I must remark though that both the English teacher and Science teachers both were a bit of a head case, but that was no big deal. The French teacher, (of course there was French, surely one of principal reasons for having chosen that school), was particularly strict and 'exigent', but due to our bilingual upbringing, we were both the best in our respective classes, and hence the teacher's favourites.

Here I suppose I should mention, Jay a little. He totally and utterly surprised me. Not more than two hours after arriving, (in the afternoon), he appeared at dinner, already surrounded by a group of his age, waved to me and went a sat to eat on the other side of the dining room.

I only found out some time later, that his first act on arriving was to hunt out the 'tuck shop' (sweet shop), trade in a hefty bundle of cash for sweets, and having bought a swagger bag load of goodies, then he shamelessly passed round the playground, buying anyone and everyone that was open to being bought; hence his immediate and impressive popularity.

I hadn't realised that my fragile, little brother, hadn't passed through J.J.'s influence, totally unscathed.

Admittedly, I found it somewhat harder to make friends, but most the boys were open and friendly, and, little by little, I sort of fell into friendships.

Strangely enough, the two boys that I came closest to at St. Josephs' were neither of my age, Duncan and Mike.

Duncan was a huge, gangling redhead, although, later on, he had no shortage of female admirers, so he couldn't have been that ugly. However, for me, if anything, he looked like an octopus that had learned how to walk upright, wearing a fluffy, orange bobble cap, neither his arms nor his legs seemed to have proper bones.

He would slowly swoosh from one place to another. He came from the town of Stornoway, which is a big town on the Isle of Lewis, in the Outer Hebrides off the North West coast of Scotland.

He once explained to me that the church used to be so powerful there, that they succeeded to close down one of the biggest hotels of the island, because it refused to bar locals from coming in to drink on Sundays.

I asked him if he was a practicing Christian, and he answered, smiling, that he needed all the practice that he could get.

Duncan was a year older than me, but he sought me out and befriended me. I once inquired what it was that had attracted him to me, 'I used to take in stray dogs, when I lived on the island, as we are not allowed to have dogs in the school, I had to settle for you'. I do admit that the response vexed me, no little, but I was also touched by this clear, open act of kindness.

Mike was, if anything, the total opposite of Duncan; he was blond, small and squat. Angelique once asked me to describe him.

I reflected that if you take the image of the perfect German youth with blond hair, blue eyes, slightly full lips, and squash him down to two thirds of his original size, add the merest hint of bulldog, then you would have a passable idea of how Mike looks!

Mike was at St. Josephs' on a scholarship, he was both intelligent and hard-working and although he was nearer Jean Jacque's age than mine, he was in my year. He would never freely admit why he became my friend, but alcohol is a great tongue loosener. So quite some years later, during one long night of heavy drinking, when we had just stolen the company, from our supposed best friend, I asked him again the question.

'Because you're a bastard! You have always been a bastard, and you'll always be one. I could smell you, even then, you were the type of guy that would haul himself, right to the top, by grabbing the balls of the guy above you, and pulling, and pulling and pulling.' I think that it was at that point that he passed out and we, (the bar staff and I), had to drag him out and into a taxi, to send him home.

It was only when I got back to my own handsome apartment that the weight of his words sunk in.

Yes I was a bastard, what I had just done might surely seem unforgivable, but I had not always been one, it was not my fault that I had arrived there, somewhere, he had forced me to act as I had.

And after all, hadn't I done it all for love?

But here, I'm getting ahead of myself….

The first year at St. Josephs' passed strangely well, Duncan and Mike became my regular companions', Duncan being a year older than me, (nearly three years for Mike), he seemed to well know his way round the school, on many levels…

It took me some years to work out Duncan's real, if unconscious motivation to be with me, and to a lesser degree, Mike.

Duncan was fundamentally a good, honest person, a good Christian in all senses of the term. The problem was, he didn't want to be, he wanted to be a rogue, a villain, a wide-boy.

He wanted, as Marie Madeleine would say, to do 'bêtises', tricks, strokes, cons, fast-ones'.

Only he couldn't bring himself to do these things, not on his own, anyway, which is way he needed us.

Duncan knew his way round St. Josephs', he knew the building well enough, but he also knew the people; the house masters and mistresses, the care taker, the grounds man, even the cook and the cleaners. He knew them all and they all knew him.

Duncan, the nice, quiet boy, who didn't seem to have many friends, but was always available to talk and help out if anyone should be in need.

What nobody else knew, was that he hated that image, he was sick of being the good boy that he always had been. In his deepest heart of hearts, he just needed to break the rules, to feel that he really was alive.

And so we did.

The three of us, (and admittedly, from time to time, we would include, Jay, if we needed someone small or from his year), would raid the larder and create midnight feasts, we introduced cigarettes to juniors, smuggled in alcohol, (only a few cans of beer, from time to time, but it was banned and therefore very daring).

Of course, the biggest and worst thing that we ever did, and for which Duncan almost got expelled from school for, was the end of year, unofficial party, where, not only did we smuggle in cigarettes and beer, but also some of the girls from the local village.

I don't exactly know how the director found out about our party, although there were enough boys there for any idiot to have let something slip, but soon after, we were all instructed to go to his office.

He looked like he had swallowed a hand full of hot chilli peppers, his face was as red as a beet's and he seemed to have steam coming out of all the holes in head, (that makes five).

'And just what do you think by bringing in cigarettes, alcohol and girls onto the school grounds?' he bellowed.

'Err, sorry sir, what are you talking about?' I thought that I should make a play for it.

'Don't make me laugh, you know exactly what I am talking about.'

'It was all my fault, sir,' you could always depend on Duncan to take the blame.

'And just how was it all your fault, Mr. McCloud?'

'I have never had the opportunity to participate in that sort of party, sir, and when the other two suggested that we go into town and purchase sweets and cakes, I just sort of lost my head, and bought the cigarettes and the beer and invited the girls too. Pierre-Alain and Mike are guilty to have helped organise the party, yes, but as to all the other stuff, that was only me.'

Sure, it sounded convincing enough, and we two were more than ready to corroborate his version of the events, after all, it got us both off the hook, but what was going to happen to Duncan?

'Very well, you two can go, I'll see that you get plenty of detention, and you can fold the counterpanes for the whole of next term.

Folding counterpanes, (the covers off the beds), was a job that each boy, (with the help of a partner), would undertake once or twice a term. It was not hard work, but it ate rather into the free hours between tea and bedtime, not forgetting the time needed for homework.

Folding them every night for a term was a real punishment, although Mike and I certainly did our best to amuse ourselves during those evenings.

Duncan's parents were summoned to the school, and there was a very long series of interviews, both with them and then also with Duncan.

He worked to convince them that this was a type of psychological breakdown, due to a lifetime of repressed desires, coupled with the stress of the end of year exams.

I really doubt the director believed him at all, but I think that he was quite pleased, as he was also our teacher of psychology, that Duncan had absorbed enough of his teachings to come up with such an interesting explanation.

At the end, he got off with a sever warning, and the threat, that if he was ever caught doing ANYTHING wrong, then he would be 'out on his ear', 'an' sae swith awaby', which is to say, that he'd back home before his feet would touch the ground.

In any case, Duncan had succeeded to find a way to finish his last year at St. Josephs', rather than have to live down being expelled. Unfortunately that meant that he would have to return to his 'good-boy' persona for the rest of his time with us. (And one that he never again succeeded to drop, hence the terrible ending of our relationship).

Chapter 5

The Big Brother

The summer would have been great, only Angelique had somehow won a competition to go and work in a children's camp in Canada, for the whole of the summer.

I suspected that my parents had something to do with it, but I couldn't prove anything, and anyway, Angelique was so happy to go, that I couldn't be that angry, even if it was just a strategy to keep us apart.

I spent more time with Jay that summer than ever before, and we spent most of it hanging out, in our favourite 'secret' place, in and around the great oak, by the river, drinking beer and smoking cigarettes.

We were careful to pass by Marie Madeleine's before going home, she was a very willing 'complice' to our 'bêtises', she would spray air freshener all over our hair and clothes, we would clean our mouths and teeth thoroughly, and would swear on the heads of all the saints, that we had spent the whole day with her, helping with tasks around the house and garden.

In our innocence, we thought that we were getting away with it; Maman never said a word, although, to tell the truth, we rarely saw her, and J.J., who seemed to be more and more often, more and more deeply drunk, seemed oblivious to everything, until one day…

'Pierre-Alain?'

'Yes, sir?'

'I've run out of smokes, your mother has forgotten to
order my cigars.'

'Yes?'

'Give me a cigarette, will you?'

'Pardon?'

'What's your problem, don't I give you enough clink, to tap ya dad a snout?' I could see that he was starting to get irritated, something in the exchange just made me freeze.

I was so shocked that he had found out, and I was so trying desperately to think up some way out, that I was not realising that it was my lack of reaction that was winding me up.

'Here dad,' Jay had once again come to my rescue, he fished into my pocket, where he know I kept the packet, and handed it to him.

'Thank you Jean Jacques, and,' he turned menacingly to me, 'don't ever let your mother know that you are bringing cigarettes into this house,' and with that, he grabbed a heavy cut glass cigarette lighter from the hall table, lit up and left the house.

'Et il est parti, sous la pluie, sans une parole, sans me regarder'.So he left, under the rain, without a word, without looking at me….

Chapter 6

A Disciplinary Interview

The next term wasn't nearly as much fun with Duncan under the constant threat of expulsion, however, Mike and I still managed to appear often enough in the local village, to be known as the 'neds', roughly translated as the hooligans.

Once the director even convoked my father, actually, both parents were invited for a 'discussion' about my relationship to discipline and school rules, but Maman cried off, using a 'very important' charity event as her excuse.

So I found myself in the 'big' office, with my father, absent mindedly puffing on a very big, expensive cigar, (surely not generally accepted), as the director explained to him, in that slow, simplified, style of language that one uses for the intellectually underprivileged, how it was not within the rules for students to decide for themselves to leave the school grounds without first seeking permission from the person responsible.

'Right,' my father suddenly seemed to return to the same realm as us, 'do you have an ash tray?' he vaguely waved his cigar towards the director, displaying an impressive head of ash, precariously perched on its end, ready to dust the ancient carpet at the merest vibration.

The director jumped forward with his office rubbish bin, in which he deftly caught the pile of ash, as it slipped from the cigar, heading for the expensive rug.

'Thank you,' he smiled in a relaxed, friendly fashion, 'so, what seems to be the problem, would be a lack of appropriate communication. Pierre-Alain.'

He turned in my direction: 'Next time that you plan to go into the village, please don't forgot to inform the appropriate employee.'

And with that, he smiled again, got up, shook the director's hand, turned and left.

The director, a little nonplussed, could think of nothing else to do but dismiss me, and gently close his office door.

Mike's parents never, ever came to the school, all they were concerned about is whether or not his scholarship was in danger, and as the school would be too embarrassed to throw out a scholarship student just because he was sneaking off into the local village without permission, as long as his exam results remained satisfactory, they would leave him alone.

As far as the academic side was concerned, many of the other students came from rich families, who had chosen an out of the way, expensive but unknown school, so as to house their slightly academically challenged offspring, until they could reasonably place them in a non-executive, non-destructive yet impressively titled position in one of their least important enterprises.

Which, in short, means to say, the expected grades were not at genius level, everyone always passed.

However, to attract the moneyed families, the school did actually have a decent teaching staff.

As Mike and I were not only intelligent, but had a real thirst for knowledge, and in total contradiction with our almost total disrespect for any and all of the school rules, we invested time in our studies, and were definitely expected to enter and succeed our 'highers'.

Chapter 7

A Short Ski Run

The winter holidays arrived and unexpectedly our parents decided that we should both learn to ski, and so the whole family packed up and left for Switzerland for the whole Christmas holiday season.

We ended up staying in the Grand Hotel in Montreux, J.J., for some unknown reason had expected that the Montreux jazz festival was some form of continual event, and he could ski during the day and listen to jazz in the evenings.

The hotel manager helpfully suggested that he make a reservation for next July, to guarantee a room.

As Montreux is on Lake Geneva, we had to travel every day to a place called Villars which took nearly an hour every day, taking a train then a bus then a ten minute walk, it was the last time that Maman allowed J.J. to plan anything.

It was a strangely harmonious holiday, both our parents, (to our total surprise), could ski passably well, while we were both total beginners.

The fact that we only saw each other over breakfast and supper, and everyone was constantly exhausted, might have tempered the meetings somewhat....

That's all that can be said about that.

Chapter 8

Bad news

It only occurred to me on returning to school that I hadn't had one moment to see Marie Madeleine nor Angelique over the holidays, and maybe the skiing trip had more than the purpose of us taking a skiing holiday as a family.

It was then that I decided that when the Easter holidays arrived, I would insist that I spend time with my two favourite females, no matter what machinations my parents would imagine to try to keep us apart, but tragically that wasn't to be.

It was a Tuesday morning, I was in maths class. We were learning to calculate the angle of friction for moving objects on rough surfaces, when the school secretary politely tapped on the door and entered without waiting for the teacher, Mrs Waters, to invite her in.

She went up to her and they spoke for about a minute, I had the sneaking suspicion that they were talking about me as the sec. glanced once or twice in my direction.

I started to feel rather uncomfortable, racking my brains to try and remember what particular 'bêtises' I had been up to the last few days and what they might have found out.

'Mr Ferguson, please will you accompany Ms. Broun to the principal's office?' I started to slowly tidy my books together, desperately trying to buy myself some time to think up excuses for stuff that I might or might not have done, and that they might or might not have found out about.

'Leave your books Pierre-Alain, Michael will collect them for you.'

Mike looked at me and nodded, but wait a minute, if I was being called to the director's office, why not also Mike, everything that I'd done recently, he had done it too?

I thought to wait a little longer to see if Mrs. Waters would send him off with me, but of course she wouldn't, she had just told him to tidy my books for me.

My head swimming from trying to understand what was going on, and still trying to make up useless excuses, I headed towards the big office.

Only to find, sitting stiffly outside, who else, but Jay.

'What's going on, James?' He and J.J. were the only people to call me James, he seemed very nervous.

'I don't know.'

'Do you think that something's wrong?'

'They wouldn't call us out of class if there wasn't'.

'Do you think that …' At that moment the door of the office opened and the director beckoned us inside.

'I have had a call from your parents', at the moment that he uttered the word parents, I could feel a huge tension leave from my brother's body, and an important release of air, at least they were both okay. 'They say that someone quite close to the family has suddenly died, and that you are both to leave on the next available train, to assist to the funeral.

'But who is it sir?' I could be polite when appropriate.

'I'm sorry Pierre-Alain, but they didn't think to inform me of any more details, you'll just have to wait until you arrive to find out. My condolences to you both. You will of course be excused all homework until you return, but the course work will necessarily have to be caught up.'

And so, without further ado, we packed a few belongings and set out, not knowing what we were heading into. 'The Charge of the Light Brigade' flooded into my mind:

'Theirs not to reason why,
Theirs but to do and die:
Into the valley of Death
Rode the six hundred.'

We hardly spoke during the trip down, each lost in his own world; I was reading 'To Kill a Mocking Bird', which I'd chosen for a book report, and Jay was reading something about robots by Asimov.

J.J. met us at the station. His face was grim. He had this rather unpleasant reaction to any form of sad news; he would get angry.

The sadder the news, the angrier he'd get. Looking at his face now, I could have imagined that all his workers had gone on strike and his businesses had gone bankrupt, but of course, I knew better.

As usual, it is Jay that sorted out the problem, 'who's died?' He asked it in as matter of fact a way as possible.

'M'r'y M'd'l'ne', my father mumbled and turned away.

Surely I hadn't heard right, he was mumbling after all.

'Marie Madeline?' Jean Jacques repeated, just to be clear.

'She's dead, get ye' cases in the boot, your mother's expecting us with supper'. And that was all he said for the rest of the evening.

I said nothing. For the first time in my life I didn't respond to Maman's 'bonsoir', I said nothing at supper, eating nothing, just toying with the food on my plate.

Thankfully no one spoke to me, or made any remark of my not eating.
Maman made small talk with Jean Jacques about school stuff and then launched into an immensely boring explanation about some special charity event that she was planning and that was to be held in some big hall off Regent's Street in some close, future moment.

J.J. ate nothing, but that was becoming more the rule than the exception. However, this once, he managed to empty a whole decanter of Scotch, which Alice had go and refill, before she went to get the coffee.

I took that occasion to look directly at him and give him an imploring stare. He responded with a slight nod, I checked that Maman had registered the exchange, she confirmed by wishing me a 'bonne nuit', and I silently made my way back up to my bedroom.

When the emotions are overtaxed, like many circuit systems, they blow a safety fuse, and then temporarily close down.

I had become an automaton; I expressed less feelings than the robots in Jean Jacque's book.

For a while, I just sat on my bed. The very same bed, (although no longer in the same room), that for all my early years, every single night, without ever missing once.

She would come, tuck me in, brush the mad cat lick of hairs off of my forehead, squeeze my left hand in hers, look into my eyes, fill me with gentle, love and care, dit, 'bonsoir, mon p'tit ange', and melt away into the night.

By some mental functioning, it was if I could see the whole scene being played out, but not from where I was sitting but from several different viewpoints all at the same time.

That it was so totally weird, even impossible, didn't strike me at all, at the time, I was totally lost in the memories....

Chapter 9

A Heavy Morning

I must have fallen asleep, but I have no memory of it, nor of the person, (J.J. I discovered later), who undressed me, and put me to bed.

I got up, and as if, still in some sort of a dream, I started to repeat the actions that I had done, all the days of my young life. Numbly rehearsing my ancient ways in a blur of forgetfulness, but today the ritual brings no comfort.

Today the kindest person in the world lies dead, and I must continue on alone, without her softness, without her love.

I came down the stairs, I was calm, quiet, self-contained. It seemed as if nothing was different, Maman was sitting at the table. She still had one half of her morning croissant on her plate.

J.J. was well into a large plate of bacon, eggs and sausage, it was often his main meal of the day, so breakfast could be quite a sumptuous repas for him.

'Good morning, Pierre-Alain, you must be hungry, I'll call for Alice to make something solid,' he was in quite a good humour.

'Bonjour mon ange, asseyez-vous', even Maman was polite and friendly.

Jean Jacques looked up from his plate of toast and jam. He must have noticed something the others didn't, something that even I wasn't aware of until a few seconds later.

'I hate you!!!', I screamed at the top of my voice,

'You're all selfish bastards!' And with that, I turned round and left the dining room, ostentatiously slamming the door as hard as I possibly could. I continued out of the house, sat down on the front steps and started to sob uncontrollably.

Some moments later, the front door opened and someone came out, I didn't look to see who it was.

The man, I could make out that he was wearing trousers from my bent posture, sat down next to me. He didn't move again, nor did he speak.

After some more time, things were quite hazy for me, I felt the flood of tears begin to run out, and more through curiosity than anything else, I raised and turned my head to see exactly who was my solitary audience member.

It was J.J. sitting patiently there, waiting, with a full glass of whiskey, (I could smell it from there), silently contemplating the driveway.

I remember feeling totally disgusted, here he was, just after breakfast with his bloody cut glass tumbler, full of alcohol, he couldn't even cope until after the funeral.
He noticed my movement.

'Here, I think that might need this,' he thrust the glass under my nose, and wrapped my hand round the heavy object, 'drink it down, laddie, ya' need to pull you'self' together.'

I nodded numbly, added my other hand to the task and poured the bitter sweet fire down my aching throat.

'Good, now go and wash up, we should be leaving already, it wunna do t' be late.' He seemed to be losing the bit of English accent that he had.

I directed the glass in his direction, he took it off me, and I turned back into the house to prepare to bid my last farewell to the one that I had loved dearly, more dearly than the spoken word can tell.

The day should have been cold, damp, windy, even raining, for that was how I was feeling, and how it usually is in books and films. In fact, it was a quite pleasant morning, the church was surprisingly full, I had not realized that she had managed to create such a wide circle of friends and close acquaintances.

I did not notice Angelique either in the church or the cemetery, in truth, I didn't really think to look.

We sat and stood together as a family, it might have been the only time that we stayed that close for longer than it would take to capture a family photo.

My parents had booked the village hall and Maman had organized the catering, I honestly don't remember anything about it.

I suppose as the closest family members it would have been normal for people to express their condolences; yet considering the relationship of employers and nanny and that most of those there were also the employees of J.J., I don't believe that anyone thought to say anything to them, let alone to little ol' me.

J.J. and Maman behaved as they always did when inviting the workers or townspeople, (more or less the same thing), to a village or work event, that is to say, they were present, friendly, but just a little aloof.

I was under the impression that no-one was taking any notice of me at all, until, out of the corner of my eye, I spied Jean Jacques, hovering some feet away, seemingly intent on discovering if there was some microscopic aquatic creature hiding in his half empty glass.

However, on closer inspection, what he was resolved to discover was whether or not the abominable Mr. Pierre-Alain Hyde, was about to resurface or not.
I carelessly picked up an alcoholic drink at random and strolled, elegantly over to my sibling.

'I'm okay.'

'You weren't okay this morning.'

'You don't understand, do you?'

'No,' he shook his head in a doleful way.

'I will never forgive them.'

'Who?'

'Them, J.J. and Maman.'

'But what have they done?'

'They kept me away from Marie Madeleine.'

'Kept you away?' He really hadn't got it.

'They have been keeping me away from Angelique, but to do that, they also kept me away from Marie Madeleine', I could see the penny dropping.

'The skiing holiday.'

'...was to keep us apart. And that would have been the last Christmas that she was alive, and she spent it alone. Her last Christmas on earth, and I wasn't there to share it with her.'

'James, it's okay, it's okay,' he was starting to get worried, he could see and hear the emotions starting to well up in me once again. 'Why don't we get out of here, and go for a walk?'

'It's okay, I'll be fine, but maybe, I'll just get some fresh air, smoke a cigarette, go for a walk.'

'Would you like for me to go with you?'

'I'll be fine, just don't tell anybody anything, not even that we've spoken.'

'You're sure?'

'Please, I just need to be alone for a while.'

'I'm here if you need me.'

'I know,' we smiled at each other, a total trust.

Such a pity that such a beautiful thing was to be smashed and broken, like a lifeless child's doll; a beautiful, broken, Barbie.

Chapter 10

Bitter - Sweet

I left the hall, broke out a fresh packet and stroked the rough wheel of the lighter's flint.

I had no plans as of where to go, I just started walking and allowed my legs to take me where they chose. To anyone with any intelligence, it would have been totally obvious where I was going to end up. Marie
Madeleine's little cottage was the same as always, the rose bushes, empty of blooms at this time of year, were as usual, the same curtains, the same songs playing on the …

How could that be? Was there someone already taken over her house? But why would they be playing her favourite songs? I rushed up to the front door, it wasn't locked. I flung it open and charged straight into the tiny front living room.

There was someone there, she had put on the music, she was sitting, huddled up on one of the old padded armchairs, softly crying.

She must of heard me coming in, a charge of elephants might have been more discrete, but she didn't look up, she didn't even move. I stopped, just for the tiniest of moments, then she was in my arms, and we cried.

Holding and being held, sharing a moment of deep, deep sadness, is one of the most wonderful experiences that I have ever known.

The short, winter's day was starting to draw in, we hadn't moved for quite a while, we more than likely had cried ourselves to sleep, safe and protected in each other's arms, and within the soothing walls of Marie Madeleine's secure fortress.

We were tightly bound together, our loss and confusion, meant that we had to hold onto each other, because there was no-one else who could understand, maybe nobody else even really cared.

I had never held anyone quite so tight, nor so close, each head nestled on the shoulder of the other.

Gently she pulled her head away, my body mirrored her movement, as we still had our arms wrapped around each other, when we came to look at each other, face to face, our heads were only inches apart.

Our noses were almost touching, are lips were almost touching, it took just the merest tilt of our necks, and we were kissing.

Not the kiss of two shy teenagers, but the deep, intense kiss of two lost souls who had suddenly found the magic balm with which to heal themselves, the secret domain where their pain was prohibited to enter.

I have had sex, many, many times in my life, with women of almost every size, shape, colour and nationality....

That night with Angelique was not sex, it was not even what I would call love making, it was much, much deeper than that.

It was a union, a joining on the most fundamental level, it was completion, the first, and terribly, the only time in my entire life that I felt whole.

What-ever bits of a human being or a soul, I lack; there she was, ready, willing and able to offer it to me.

Again we slept, and I suppose we would have slept even longer if there had not been that discrete knocking on the bedroom door.

'Pierre-Alain, J.J. and Maman are going nuts. When you didn't come back last night, they thought that maybe you'd jumped off a bridge or something. They would have called the police, but Maman was concerned that it would cause a scandal.'

'How did you know where to find me?'

'I could have guessed that you we here all along.'

'But why didn't you come before?'

'I reckoned that you'd come home when you were ready, it was just taking bit too long. Sorry to have to disturb you. Hi, Angelique, nice to see you again.'

Trying not to look too obviously at her half naked torso, hastily covered up, as best she could when he had entered, he smiled at us both and turned towards the door.

'I'll wait for you downstairs.'

The story was that he had gone out to find me, looking round the village, he had stumbled on me, sleeping off an excess of alcohol, drunk on an empty stomach, while in a pretty emotional state, propped up, on the tombstone of Marie Madeleine.

The story seemed reasonable, and everyone was happy to believe it, until it became all too obvious that the night had not passed exactly according to that specific version.

This, I was not to find out until some months later….

Chapter 11

Back to School

In the meantime, Jean Jacques and I were quietly returned to St. Joseph's, and life returned pretty much back to normal, except for one or two particular experiences.

The first was an unsuccessful experience of what one must admit to name as homosexuality. In the reality of the thing, it was much, much less than that.

We slept in small dorms of four boys of more or less the same age. As I was pretty mature for my years, I ended up sleeping with some boys of the final year.

Since returning from home, I had been pretty 'sage', well behaved. In fact, I had little energy for anything much, as if all my energy had been drained out from me.

With the loss of Marie Madeleine, I had already part of my soul ripped out of my, still young body, but with the passing connecting with Angelique, another, even greater part of my being, had been left in her tender arms.

I had neither smoked nor drank nor escaped into the village in those following weeks. Then, one night, quite late on, after the others must have been asleep, for no apparent reason, the boy, almost a year older than me, name of Peter, quietly slipped out of his bed, which was next to his, and asked me if I wanted to come over to his bed.

I hesitated for a moment, but then reflecting of just how deeply lonely I was feeling, I thought, 'why not?', got out of my bed, and into his own.

He sort of took me into his arms, if I closed my eyes, maybe I could make myself believe it was Angelique. His face, softly brushed against mine, but where her face was soft and velvety smooth, his was already bristly and rough. He tilted his head back and twisted it slightly towards me, his mouth was only inches from mine.

As I had not smoked or drunk in weeks, I couldn't escape from the awareness that had partaken of both, and no long ago neither, (maybe that is what motivated him, or at least gave him the courage to ask me). I turned my face away as if to protect myself from being contaminated by his fowl breath and unpleasant desires.

It was enough to prove to myself, that I certainly wasn't homosexual.

'Sorry, I have to go back to bed.'

'Okay', strangely enough he didn't seem at all put out by my rejection, maybe he was just experimenting as well, as was somewhere relieved that it hadn't gone any further. I was never to know, as we never ever spoke of the event, it was if it never happened.

The other event, much more flattering to my ego, was that the director asked my parents if they would allow me to take my maths higher exam a year early.

The reason for this, was Duncan was the only boy in his year capable of taking the maths exam, that year, the others had all dismally failed their mock exams in February.

However, even Duncan was still far from certain to pass, so the director felt it would be better for him to have someone to study with.

I, in all modesty, was a bit of a maths wiz, and was already, unofficially, studying the same syllabus. It was quickly agreed, and from then on, Duncan and I found ourselves as study-mates for maths, which only re-enforced an already strong connection.

We both studied hard those last few months, even choosing to stay over the Easter holidays so as to give ourselves the best chance for the summer exam session.

Looking back, with the clarity that time brings to the picture, I have begun to question the version of events as written above.

It now seems all too convenient that I was needed to support Duncan with that exam, so much so that I had to stay at school over those holidays.

Much, much too convenient….

Chapter 12

Quisling

Jean Jacques returned from home a different person.

We both had our own groups of friends, both for study and for leisure, but we would still, from time to time, hang out for an afternoon, take some smokes, (yes I was smoking again), and some drinks, (beer or cider for preference), go for a stroll to the edge of the school grounds, and share some time.

Some-times we had things to talk about, school, home, girls, what-ever.

Jean Jacques avoided me.

It wasn't so obvious to begin with, it was normal that he had stuff to do and catching with his usual crowd, but as he had just returned from home, I thought that he would pass some time the first week-end, to bring me up to speed with any family or village gossip.

I was also particularly keen to know if he had any news from Angelique.

(We had long since decided not to write to each other, as we suspected that either my father or my mother were both capable to pressure the village postman to first deliver any mail, coming or going from either of us, into their manicured, eager hands).

The first week-end came and went, as did the second one.

I then began to become aware that when-ever I came into a room or the recreation yard and he was there, before I might have time to get close enough to talk to him, he had already disappeared.

That is all that can be said....

Chapter 13

Father knows best

It was only when I returned home for the summer holidays that finally the pieces of the puzzle started to fall into place – Angelique was gone!

'Where is she?!' I screamed, as charged back into the house, noisily slamming the front door.

'Pierre-Alain, ça ne va pas.'

'Where is she?' I wasn't to be distracted by her demand for politeness.

'She's away', his glass was half empty, but there was no way to know if it was his first, second, fifth or tenth.

'Where is she gone?' Maman looked to J.J., it wasn't often that she looked to him for support.

'Sit down, son', his tone was gentle, it was a polite invitation, but there was no way that I would be able to refuse.

Out of the corner of my eye I noticed a movement of something, should I be more precise, someone, escaping up the stairs – the coward, le lâche!

'Would you like a drink?' Maman sniffed, she had not yet come to accept us drinking anything other than a small glass of good wine with our evening meals.

J.J. swept an authoritative glance over her, this was not the usual way that things happened in our house, Maman had almost total control over our rights and obligations, J.J. almost never, ever interfered.

'Here,' he handed me one of his heavy, cut glass tumblers, 'ice?'

'Sure, thanks.'

'Angelique is pregnant.' I almost dropped my glass.

'Do you know who the father is?' My mother could control herself no longer.

'Petit idiot, es-tu si bête que tu penses que nous ne sommes pas au courant ?'

'What are you talking about, what do I think that you are not aware of what?'

'That you are the father, what else, ya' idiot?'

'How?' I was honestly lost.

'Do ya' take us bother for idiots?'

'I'm sorry … the day of the funeral, it was the only ….'

'It only takes once.'

'But is she alright? Where is she? What's happening?'

'We offered to help her do the right thing', I think that she was speaking to me in English to be sure that I definitely understood, I had only been speaking school French for the six months.

'What do you mean, the right thing?'

'She is much too young to look after a baby.'

'You tried to get her to get rid of it?' I was feeling increasingly angry, exactly why, I was not capable to analyse, was it the idea of trying to get her abort, or keeping me in the dark, or not asking my opinion? I am still not totally clear.

'Neither she nor you are old enough to be responsible for a bairn.'

'So what have you done? You cannot force her to accept an abortion.'

'Her father could have…' J.J. gave her a rather nasty look, the sense of which I was not capable to decipher
'It was not good for her or her family, for her to stay in the village.'

Nor for you; I found myself adding under my breath.

'But where is she?', I found myself repeating for the 'x'ieme time.

'Pierre-Alain,' she came round to face me, and knelt down on one knee, in the softest voice that I have ever heard her use, ever, 'she is in a safe place. She will have the baby, and then we will do what is necessary to see that it gets placed in a good home, with people that will be able to look after it, in the very best circumstances.'

'Came, drink up son, it's about time you got to know something about our factory that you are going to take over, some-time soon. It'll get your mind off this trouble, then we can stop off at the 'Hounds', on the way back, and relax a while.

And so the discussion ended. There was nothing more to be said for the moment. I allowed myself to led out by J.J., into his old Jaguar, the one with the two petrol tanks, of which only the gauge of the left one worked, the right one, was named, 'the mystery tank', as he was never sure how much was left in it.

He gave me a mini tour of the works, it was much too hurried for me to register much, but then again, it was only an excuse, and we were both aware of that, so it was okay.

We stopped, as planned, and I got rather drunk before we finally got back home.

Maman informed us that Jean Jacques had a bit of a headache, so he wasn't to be joining us for dinner that night.

Jean Jacques knew, he had known since the Easter holidays, and he had kept that knowledge from me. This was not going to be forgiven, or forgotten, ever, and it wasn't.

We returned to St. Joseph's as usual, he tried to start several conversations on the trip up, but I had nothing to say to him.

The two brothers that were always there to support and protect the other, no longer existed, now it was 'chacun pour soi', each one for themselves.

So if that was the way that it was going to be, then that was the way it would be.

Chapter 14

Back to School Final Year

I returned to St Joseph's to be congratulated on passing the maths exam, however, not with the highest marks.

My parents must surely have also had this result, but with the conflict over Angelique and the baby, they either forgot to tell me, or, more than likely, never found an appropriate moment to share the good news.

Jean Jacques came up and tried to congratulate me, but I had no time for him. As I turned away from him, I could see the tears starting to well up in his eyes, but he had had his chance with me, and he had blown it.

One treason too many me lad, one treason too many.

Even when Marc Anthony proclaimed that Brutus was an honorable man, we all knew what he really meant.

I hoped that by passing the maths last year, I'd be excused this year, but the director would have none of it.

It seems that we were taught the very minimum so that Duncan would pass the exam, this year I was to complete the curriculum correctly, and hopefully pass, this time, with a more respectable mark.

As I really did like maths, I didn't mind that much, and as Mike being over a year younger than everyone else, sometimes had to stretch to keep up, I could be there to help him a bit.

After all with Duncan leaving and Jean Jacques having defected to the enemy, Mike was the only real friend that I had left.

The winter term played out uneventfully, I wasn't really in the mood for much messing about, and Mike was having to really study to prepare for his final year exams.

I was looking forward to the Christmas holidays with both excitement and trepidation, would Angelique be there?

Would my parents try to keep me from seeing her? What of the baby, would it have already have been adopted?

Would there be any why to found out what had happened to it?

Not once did it cross my mind that anything bad could have happened to either of them.

Anyhow, I trusted that if there had been any really bad news, I would have been informed.

Chapter 15

Mother Knows Best

My parents treated my return as if the crisis of summer had never happened.

They were slightly warmer and friendlier than usual, that was true, and they seemed honestly concerned about my choice to ignore totally my younger brother.

I wasn't sure how to bring up the subject of Angelique, Jean Jacques, who always seemed to know what I needed to know or to ask, tried to curry favor with me, by asking the question.

'Is Angelique back home yet?'

'No lad, not yet.'

'Why not?', now the subject was open, I couldn't stop myself from asking.

'Cela ne vous concerne pas'.

'Of course it concerns me, she's my girlfriend; she's had my baby!'

'Pierre-Alain, ça suffit!'

'Well?' This time I turned to J.J. as I felt that he was the weaker of the two.

'She's not here right now.'

'So where is she?'

'She's somewhere safe, somewhere where she's being looked after.'

'And the baby, what has happened to the baby?'

Maman moved as if to respond, but she didn't get the opportunity.

'The bairn is still with her mother.'

'What? She hasn't given it away yet?'

'That's been a bit of a complication.' I looked first to him, and then to my mother.

'What sort of a complication?'

'She didn't give the baby away.' Jean Jacques was trying to be helpful.

'Is there some reason that you think that you should be part of this conversation?'

'James, there's no need t' talk t' your brother like that.'

'This is my business, not his, I'd prefer that he was asked to leave.' I then stared very hard at J.J., he didn't have much choice.

'Ay, I suppose that he is right, this doesn't really concern you lad, why don't you run along and ask Alice to make us all a cup of tea?'

As for Jean Jacques, if he wasn't happy about being sent off like an employee, he was even less happy to be excluded from the conversation.

It was a small victory, but in the circumstances, I was in need of all the victories that I could muster.

'Is there anything wrong with the baby?'

'No, she's fine.'

'Oh, it's a girl, then.'

'Oui, c'est une fille.'

'Maman, please can you talk in English, I'm tired, and stressed, and you're insistence to always talk in French is pissing me off!'

Of course there was no need for that, I was perfectly capable of understanding everything that she was saying, but I was feeling so totally out of control, I just had to find a way to blow off some steam.

'Pierre-Alain, that is no way to talk to your mother, you will apologise at once.'

'Je suis désolé Maman, je m'excuse.' I know that I had gone too far, so I gave up the battle.

I left the house for a long walk and to burn up a full packet of cigarettes.

Chapter 16

Confirmation

As if I was still an object that fate was moving left or right at will, I found myself once more outside the old house, the home of Marie Madeleine.

I went, naturally up to the front door, but even before I reached that target I was stopped.

It was a voice that I knew well, for the shortest of instants, I thought it was the voice of Angelique, but it wasn't, it was that of her mother.

'It's locked.'

'Hello', I turned round to face her, in my present state, the resemblance was troubling. It was from her that
Angelique had inherited her flaming hair, and scary, green eyes. And that soft lilt of her speech was all that she had kept from her early years in the South of Ireland.

'Where is she?' The question tumbled out again, there was no stopping that.

'I can't tell you, Pierre- Alain, your father has threatened to throw Patrick out of the works and us out of this house, if I so much as talk to you about her. I am sorry'.

'I'm wanting to tell you, I'm willing to tell you, I'm waiting to tell you', I played with the words, it was all that I could do, I could see that she was telling the truth.

This dog had learnt that it was helpless, the experiment had been a success, she knew that she had no place to go, she could only wait and hope that soon the pain would soon go away.

'But they are both okay, Angelique and the baby?'

'You know that I can't tell you even that,' but as she said the words, she smiled, and ever so softly, she nodded her head, not even a nod, just a slight lowering of the chin.

And with that, she bid me good day and returned back into her little, identical house.

There was really no need to have asked her if Angelique and the baby, baby girl were alright. My parents had said as much, and I had no reason to doubt them of that, but I just wanted to have some information from somebody that was on our side.

I was terribly short on allies.

I was even tempted to make peace with Jay, but no, Jean Jacques had sided with them, he had known all along about Angelique's pregnancy and had kept it from me.

Maybe he even knows where she is, but I was sure, even if he did, he was too much a coward to tell me and assume the storm of our parent's wrath.

I walked through the soft, brown melting snow, rusting into rivers of mush. Snow….

I was momentarily taken back to Montreux, and the family holiday; the closest that we had ever seemed to be a family.

Yet it was just a lie, a simple charade to keep Angelique and me apart.

Chapter 17

Jay's Last Chance

My parents flatly refused to say anything more on the subject of Angelique or the baby.

Maman was oddly quiet, not even the usual reproaches about my table manners or use of 'rough' language.

J.J., if anything was more talkative than usual, filling the empty spaces with stories of wild times in darkest Glasgow, where, as a teenager and young adult, anything went, as long as you didn't get caught. Then again, as most of the local police knew everyone by family and by name, a good telling off and clip round the ear, was often all that would transpire.

Jean Jacques tried to join in in the conversations, if we were not at the beginning of a meal, I would simply get up and leave, otherwise I would just act as if he hadn't spoken.

After several attempts to lead me into discussions about holidays or school, he simply gave up.

I can't say it was the worst few weeks of my life, as you will see, but it was certainly the worst to date, I was more than relieved to pack my bags and return to the emotionally calm haven of St Joseph's.

At least the discipline of studying gave me the distraction that I needed, Jean Jacques had realised that I wasn't going to forgive him and gave me a wide berth, tant mieux for both of us.

I knew that if and when things would sort themselves out with Angelique and the baby, then I would surely be informed, so there was nothing to do but wait and be patient.

So I thrust myself into my studies, Mike was now my constant companion and so we studied and hung out together.

Mike was certainly intelligent; he was over a year in advance of his age, was here on a scholarship and was keeping up with the rest of our year.

However, his mind was rough, he had no finesse, no subtlety, in that I regretted my falling out with

Jay, he had an incredibly agile and flexible mind, if anything, his thinking was more refined than mine, he could see into a problem or a situation, in an instant, in a flash.

Yes, I did regret losing my little brother, but it was his fault, not mine, but yet, I was paying the price.

Easter was fast approaching and still no news from my parents that things were sorting themselves out, so I phoned the house one evening.

'Oui, 'ello.'

'Hello, it's me.'

'Attends une minute, je vais chercher ton père.' And with that she left, with me hanging like an old forgotten rag on a sagging clothes line, which no-body wants anymore, but can't be bothered to remove.

'Hello James, how you doin' laddie?' He must have been into his 4th or 5th glass already.

'I'm doing fine, listen, is there any news yet of Angelique or the baby.'

'I'm sorry lad, but it's still not sorted yet, she will no' give over the baby.'

'So what's giving to happen? When is she coming back?'

'We're still thinking on what's the best thing to do.'

'But why is it your decision, it should be hers' and mine.'

'You're both still under age, you don't yet get t' decide.'

'But you can't keep her prisoner for ever.'

'She's no a prisoner, she's bein' well looked after, they both are.'

'Are they both okay?'

'Yes they are, the little one's thriving.'

'So when can I go and see them?'

'We don't think that that is a very good idea.'

'Who doesn't think that it's a good idea?'

'Jamie, just cool down, you're much too young t'
be a father.'

'Uncle Jack', (one of J.J.'s brothers), 'was married
at my age.'

'Ay, and he never amounted to nothing.'

'But it's my baby.'

'No it's not your baby, and you'll do well to give
up on that idea. You've a whole life ahead o' you,
you don't need to be chained down here with a
scrawny bairn,'

'So you won't let me see her?'

'It's out of the question.'

'Then I won't be home for Easter.'

'That would be sad, we miss you, you know.'

'Not enough to tell me where she is and to let me see her?'
'That, son, is not negotiable'.

'Then there is nothing more to discuss.' And with that I quietly and gently hung up the phone.

I admit that in that moment of weakness I sought out Jay. He was clearly surprised and pleased that I had come over to speak to him.

'What can I do for you brother?' He asked in a jokey way.

'I need to know where Angelique and the baby are.'

'And you think that I know?'

'You seem to know most things.'

'Well I don't know that.'

'So, maybe you could find out, people talk to you.'

'People could also talk to you.'

'No, they can't, if they did, they'd lose their jobs, and maybe even their homes. You know that.'

'No, I didn't actually know, but I could have guessed.'

'So you'll do it, you'll go home at Easter and find out where they are?'

'Jamie, you know that I can't.'

'Look, I'm giving you a chance to redeem yourself.'

'To do what?'

'You heard what I said, you know about Angelique and the baby, but you didn't tell me.'

'I couldn't, I was sworn to secrecy.'

'From your own brother, don't you have any loyalty?'

'This is totally unfair.'

'I'm asking you to do something for me, something important, will you or will you not help me?'

'I've told you, I can't, please don't ask me to do that, you know that I can't.'

I had to turn away again, I couldn't cope with those same brown eyes, where mine must have been cold as flints, his were melting away, like a sad, chocolate Easter bunny, left in the warm, spring sunshine, dripping tears of dying, sweetness.

'I gave you another chance, I'll never ask you anything, ever again.' And that was the last conversation that we ever had.

Other than the announcement of my father's death, in that house of laughter, he never really tried to speak to me again, either.

Chapter 18

Dealing with the Devil

True to my word, I stayed at school during the Easter holidays.

Mike and his parents were concerned about his highers and so they negotiated for him to be able to stay over the hols. It was a little complicated with his scholarship but the director was happy to support such an application, and it got sorted out without too much problem.

I had intentionally blanked out all thoughts of Angelique and the baby, if there was nothing that I could do in the moment to sort things out, then I would just have to occupy myself otherwise until I could.

How I occupied myself was my exams, I switched off all my emotions and put all the anger and hurt into doing something useful.

Coming from two particularly stubborn parents, 'entêté' as Maman would describe us, when I put my head and charged towards something, it was rare that any obstacles could resist.

It is because of this trait that it was so frustrating to be confronted to the other members of my family, who, if nothing else, shared those similar traits.

Before I was really aware, the exams had come, and then … finished.

After that, there was nothing else to do but pack up my stuff, bid goodbye to everyone, and come home.

J.J. met us at the station, Jean Jacques had come down on the same train but had sat in different carriages, but now we were forced to share the car.

I sat in the front, the prerogative of being the oldest.

The ride home passed in silence, but as we arrived home, J.J. turned to me, 'you stay in the car, Alice will take your bags upstairs.' He opened the boot and pulled out our bags, Jean Jacques got out of the car, daring a sidelong glance, as a form of question and support, I chose to seem not to notice.

He got back into the car and restarted the engine. I waited for him to make some sign of what he wanted from me, but he just puffed on one of his big cigars and concentrated on his driving.

We arrived shortly at the pub, this meant that he wanted to talk to me, away both from Maman and Jean Jacques. It wouldn't take an Einstein to guess on what the subject would be.

He waited until we had both downed a large whiskey and were served a second before he opened.

'James, this has been a very complicated affair.'

'Only because you've made it so.'

'You need to understand, because of the works and all, we canna' have you … frequenting, this girl.'

'Her name is Angelique, as if you don't know or can't remember, unless it has something to do with this.' I gestured towards the glasses, it was a low shot, but I was already feeling that I wasn't going to appreciate this little 'chat'.

'Angelique is back home.' I seemed not to hear correctly or not to understand. I just looked at him stupidly, like when Benny, disappeared for years after entering into a broom closet, suddenly coming back, as if no time had passed.

'Come again?'

'Angelique is back home.'

'And the baby?'

'And the baby.'

'Then let's go!' I was already on my feet.

'You'll be going no-where, me lad.'

'But, she's here, here with the baby.'

'The bairn is not your child.'

'But I don't understand.'

'Drink, it helps,' I did, 'she slept with someone that was passing through the village, it was just after the funeral, she'd had too much t' drink, she was feeling very sad and lonely, he took advantage of her. Everybody understands, people have been very understanding.'

Maybe I'd already drunk too much, 'cus I wasn't understanding ; I wasn't following what he was saying.

'But you said that I was the father, that that night. Wait a minute, she couldn't have slept with someone else, she was with me.'

'You will listen, and listen well. She was taken advantage of by a passing stranger that is what happened.

Do you understand?'

Slowly, slowly the penny dropped.

'But I am the father, we know that I am, she knows.'

'She knows that her father works in my factory and she lives in one of my houses, and she knows how t' keep her gob shut.'

'Well I don't work in your fucking factory, and I'm eighteen now. Not that means anything to you, but I'm my own man, I can do what I like.'

'Sure y' can, and jest what do you plan to do, 'man'?'

'Well, I'm going to see her, to see my baby.'

'And then?'

'What do you mean, 'and then?''

'If you don't wish to do what your parents want, and as y' said, you're now a man, you can make your own decisions, but if y' choose to go out on your own, you're out on your own,'

'And just what is that meant to mean?'

'That you find yourself somewhere t' live, a job, a life.'

'Are you threatening to throw me out?' I could feel a knot tying itself, loop by loop in my throat, it was making it harder and harder to breath.

I had the impression that I was drowning, here on dry land, in this dirty, smoky pub, my head was starting to reel, had he put something into my drink. I wanted to stand, to walk out, to scream, 'fuck you!', but I could hardly sit straight.

He didn't move, other than softly sucking on his cigar, it had gone out, but he made as to have not noticed.

He would do that sometimes, allow his cigar to go out, but keep on sucking and chewing on it, a big, wet, pathetic, phallic, adult dummy.

I took the proverbial moment, breathing more calmly, getting my thoughts together, piecing the puzzle into a perfectly proportioned picture.

'You are threatening to throw me out.'

'I am allowing you to take control of your life, since that is what you want. And with control comes responsibility. You wish to go to Angelique, to take her and the baby on as your responsibility, then be my guest, go and do it. But if you choose that route, you choose it alone, and you can expect no support from us.'

'And I am supposed to just abandon her? How will she survive?'

'That is no longer your concern.' That was just too much for me.

'Yes it is my concern, I will not see her or the baby starve because of me, if I have to go and get a job in the factory to support them, I will!'

For some reason that didn't seem at all apparent in the moment, J.J. smiled, and in a very warm and friendly voice replied.

'I know you would, James, and I'm proud that you would think to make such a sacrifice, but it's no' necessary. Since Marie Madeleine passed over, we've had to close the nursery because we've had no one to run it. Angelique has very kindly agreed to take over the nursery, that way she can work and earn her own living, and look after the baby at the same time.'

'And exactly where is she going to live with my baby?'

'Where she has spent most of her time over the past years, in Marie Madeleine's house, the rent will be well within her means, and she will have her parents next door in case she needs anything.'

'But I want to go and see them.'

'By all means, go and see them, but remember, there's no coming back, not for either of you.'

'What do you mean, not for either of you?'

'Angelique has promised never to speak with you again, that way she keeps her job, her house and her baby.'

'She has agreed to that?'

'She is a reasonably intelligent young lady, she understands about making choices.'

'And she has agreed never to speak to me again?'

'Ever'.

'Can I have another drink?'

'You can have as much as you want.'

After that, the rest of the evening was a blur, I don't remember getting home, or undressing or getting into bed.

What I do remember was the devil of a headache the next morning.

Chapter 19

The Calm after the Storm

It must have been after ten when I finally made it to the dining room, Jean Jacques was just finishing a cup of coffee, and J.J. was reading a newspaper. His cup seemed empty and his cigar was out, patiently sitting in a heavy cut glass ashtray, waiting to be called again into service.

Jean Jacques downed the rest of his coffee, scowled at me and left. I was not yet used to this type of reaction from my little brother, but I soon got used to it, it became the standard form of communication between us for most of the rest of lives.

J.J. glanced up from his paper, and without a word, struck the bell.

'Alice,' he looked up as she entered, 'please make us another pot of coffee, rather strong,' he added as an afterthought.

'You look a bit rough, Jamie, I thought maybe that you could hold your liquor a bit better than that.

Still, we've the whole summer ahead of us to get you into training for Aston.'

Aston Business School, was my first choice for university and I'd been offered a fairly easy two B's and a C. It had become increasingly difficult to get into Aston these past few years, as its reputation had increased, even on the international level, they had had to up the entry grades to keep the numbers within reason.

Alice arrived with a steaming coffee jug, and I poured myself out a large cup, into which I dunked four brown sugar cubes.

I drank some of the coffee, it was good coffee, J.J. only had the best off coffees, cigars and of whiskeys, for the rest everything else was okay as it came.

I must have been what the hypnotists term as dissociated,

I was trying to work out how to react to J.J., after the heavy handed, bullying way he had treated the situation with Angelique and the baby, then supporting me in getting totally rat-assed pissed, and now his very civil attitude towards me.

Should I still be angry with him, or should I just act as if nothing had happened?

All the while that I was chewing over this problem, I must have been chewing over the plate of croissants that had been left over from everyone else's breakfast.

'I see y' got your appetite back, lad, that's a really good sign, shows that y' can get totally smashed and still function the next day, that's really important.'

Was he talking total rubbish, or was this really what he believes to be true? I was really having a hard time working all this out. So I did what I usually did in these situations, I ran away.

'Just off out for a smoke.'

'You can light one up in here, if you like.'

'No, thanks, I feel more comfortable smoking outside. I might even go for a little stroll. I'll see you later.'

'Sure, sure, a walk'll do you good!'

With that, I was out of the house, and gone….

Chapter 20

The Only Deal in Town

It didn't take me long to realize that, as usual, I was heading towards Marie Madeleine's old house. I stopped for a moment, threw my half smoked cigarette onto the floor, angrily ground it pulp with my right heel, turned and walked off in the opposite direction.

As I now had no-where else to go, I headed towards the river, but I was not the only one to have had that bright idea either.

It was one of the favourite haunts of Jay and I, since we were old enough to be considered 'sage' enough to be left to our own devices.

Considering the circumstances, it was not surprising to find him there, perched in the old, knotted broken oak, staring gloomily at the trickle of brown water, edging its sad passage down to the unpitying ocean many miles downstream.

He must have heard my coming, he might have even glanced up at my approach, but as I got close enough to see him in detail, he was, as Viola might have been, waiting in his willow cabin, for someone to call upon his soul, from within the house, but I was no Olivia, for me, he was no more than one of my nightmare doorstep, lions, he could really have been carved in stone, nothing moved, not a twitch or a muscle.

I knew not what I wished for, nor what I wanted, but I just stood there watching him, not watching me, for maybe five minutes.

He refused to move, to acknowledge my very presence.

I had an impulse to bend down, find a nice, not too heavy stone, and throw it at him, he wasn't that far away, and I would likely have got him, but I didn't.

No, I did not throw the stone, I did not shatter that glass wall that I had constructed over the last year.

No I did reach out for my brother, the one person that could have helped and comforted me in this moment of total abandon, no I didn't have the courage nor the good sense.

I did what I became good at, I turned and walked away from those that loved me, from those that I loved.

I went home and made a deal with the devil, actually I mean J.J., but it felt pretty much the same. I promised to keep away from Angelique and the baby, if he would pay for me to go and stay in New York for the rest of the summer.

He haggled for a while about how much I would have as a living allowance, but before the end of the week, I had my ticket from Heathrow.

I was on my way….

The Island of Serenity
Book 3
Pleasure

Chapter 6. The Island of Pleasure:

Faron arrives in a dream of modern day Venice, only here he can eat, drink, smoke and womanise to his heart's content, at no cost on any level.

Only he quickly realises that he has lost all ability to experience pleasure.

His guide takes him into the secret, inner world of women; to an Ancient Chinese Geisha house and a Modern Indian Ashram.

It is time to learn the painful lessons of pleasure.

What can you learn from this second island of Serenity?

Adventures with the Master

Dhargey was a sickly child, or so his parents treated him.

He was too weak to join the army or work in the fields or even join the monastery as a normal trainee monk.

To explain to the 'Young Master' why he should be accepted into the order with a lightened program, he was forced to accompany the revered old man a little ways up the mountain.

As his parents watched him leave; somewhere they felt that they would never see their sickly, fragile boy ever again, somewhere they were totally right.

He was a happy, healthy seven year old until he witnessed the riders, dressed in red and black, destroying his village and murdering his parents; the trauma cut deep into his psyche.

Only the chance meeting with a wandering monk could set him back onto the road towards health and serenity.

Through meditation, initiations, stories, taming wild horses, becoming a monkey, mastering the staff and the sword; the future 'Young Master' prepares to face his greatest demon.

Two men, two journeys; one goal...

REMEMBER

Stories and poems for self-help and self-development based on techniques of Ericksonian and auto-hypnosis

Dusk falls, the world shrinks little by little into a smaller and smaller circle as the light continues to diminish.
The centre of this world is illuminated by a small, crackling sun; the flames dance, and the rough faces of the people gathered there are lit by the fire of their expectations.

The old man will begin to speak, he will explain to them how the world is, how it was, how it was created. He will help them understand how things have a sense, an order, a way that they need to be.
He will clarify the sources of un-wellness and unhappiness, what is sickness, where it comes from, how to notice it and… how to heal it.
To heal the sick, he will call forth the forces of the invisible realms, maybe he will sing, certainly he will talk, and talk, and talk.

Since the beginning of time we have gathered round those who can bring us the answers to our questions and the means to alleviate our sufferings.
This practice has not fundamentally changed since the earliest times; in every era, continent and culture we have found and continue to find these experiences.

In this, amongst the oldest of the healing traditions, he has succeeded to meld modern therapy theories and techniques with stories and poems of the highest quality.

With much humanity, clinical vignettes, common sense and lots of humour, the reader is gently carried from situation to situation.
Whether the problems described concern you directly, indirectly or not at all, you will surely find interest and benefits from the wealth of insights and advices contained within and the conscious or unconscious positive changes through reading the stories and poems.